The Bradford Family

DATE DUE


```
jF      Jenkins, Jerry
JEN     Bradford Family:
        Good sport,      w/d
        bad sport
```

Please Return To:
GREATER PORTLAND BIBLE CHURCH
452-9375

© 1985 by
JERRY B. JENKINS

Moody Press Edition 1990

ISBN: 0-8024-0810-9

1 2 3 4 5 6 Printing/LC/Year 94 93 92 91 90

Printed in the United States of America

To Eric, Celeste, David, Jennifer,
Joshua, and Timothy

Contents

1

The Big Race

Daniel Bradford's Malta XG bicycle was in the middle of the pack as he raced through the half-mile dirt course. The early July sun had risen bright and hot. It had turned the soft course into a dry, dusty, brick-hard ordeal.

Daniel wished he could open his mouth wider to breathe more deeply. But the chin strap of his helmet was too tight. He didn't know why he had to wear a crazy helmet anyway.

Sure, he'd fallen before. But he'd never hit his head. He had begun racing six weeks before. Of all the spills he had seen, none had resulted in a serious injury. One sprained wrist was all he'd seen. And that was a girl in the younger kids' competition.

He sneaked a quick look behind him. He and the six cyclists ahead of him had finally separated themselves from the rest of the pack. This quarter final qualifying heat was two laps. He had to finish in the top five to get into the semifinals.

He felt good and strong, but a little short of breath. He'd never made the semifinals before. He put his left foot out to guide himself around a tight turn. But all the riders ahead of him had done the same, and he was riding their dust.

He could still see fairly well. The dust just settled on his face mask and didn't get in his eyes. As soon as he was on the straightaway again, he stood and pumped furiously. When his legs ached from the effort, he sat back down but kept pedaling. Quickly he wiped the dust from his face mask with his gloved hand.

The riders flew past the starting point and started their second lap. Daniel could hear all the parents and friends cheering and calling out their encouragement. He wanted to see his family, but he didn't dare look for them.

The first obstacle on the course, after the riders had picked up as much speed as possible, was a steep incline and a jump. That jump whipped the bikes sideways in the air and brought the riders down with a thud.

The secret was to get straightened out in the air. If a bike hit sideways, the wheels quit spinning, and the bike would flop over, usually in the path of the other riders. All the earlier races, while Daniel was just learning, had been on damp days. The ground had been soft and sometimes even muddy.

On those kinds of days, the jump was fun. It had been scary at first, but the officials had walked the kids through the course. They let them do it slowly, let them do it alone, and let them get used to it. And even in the races—especially on the first lap when thirty riders might go over the jump in three or four seconds—it was scary but fun.

That was because the landing was soft. Even if you flipped over, you couldn't get too badly hurt by being run over. Most of the riders knew how to avoid you. Daniel fell in his second race. The rider behind him swerved around him and fell himself. The rider behind *him* ran over his elbow. But the fallen rider just jumped up and got back into the race.

Today, though, Daniel didn't want to fall. He was in seventh place. No one was close enough behind him to challenge him. And he felt he had a good chance to finish in the first five. What a thrill that would be!

He didn't expect to win the finals. No way. Randy Hickock would win that—just as he would win the other quarter final heat. And just as he would win the semifinal. He was so much better than everyone else that it almost wasn't fair.

Randy was a thin, wiry, dark-haired kid. At twelve he was a year older than Daniel. And he was experienced. He had moved into the area from California. His jacket was plastered with all kinds of patches that told of the various records he held and all the tournaments he had won.

In fact, in California, he claimed, he was so good that he was pushed into the class for thirteen- to fifteen-year-olds. And he had still won several trophies. He was mad that in his new city and state they wouldn't move him up to the next class.

As far as the other kids were concerned, it would have been just fine if he had moved up. No one else could win with Randy Hickock in the race. He hadn't lost one heat since he started early in June. In fact, he was so good that he could fool around during the race. He could get behind on purpose, slow down, make people go around him, and still win.

Sometimes he would ride in third place for half the race. Then he would speed to the front and get about a fifty-foot lead. Then he would slow down and bend over, looking at his bike as if something was wrong. The crowd would scream. And the second- and third- and fourth-place riders pushed as hard as they could to catch him. But he would casually straighten up and speed up just in time to hold them off at the end.

Daniel was glad not to be in the same heat with him now. He knew most of the other riders. They were all good guys who wouldn't try any cute tricks that might hurt someone. It wasn't that they weren't tough, talented riders. If

9

Daniel tried to pass them on the inside on a turn, or on the outside on the straightaway, they would speed up and move into his path.

There was nothing wrong with that. It was all part of the sport. If you were in front, you could ride anywhere you wanted. In road racing or Olympic-style racing, you could not crowd someone unless your whole bike was ahead of him.

No one in this type of racing wanted to hurt anybody, Daniel thought. Not even Randy Hickock. But if you tried passing him without enough speed to get by, he'd run you off the course. There were ways to defend yourself. Slowing down or hitting the brakes was the best way. Then he would angle off in front of you, and you could slip back in behind him.

There were lots of ways to pass someone, and Daniel had passed many. But never Randy.

Daniel stood and pumped hard. They were pedaling through the fastest part of the course. He wanted to pass the number six rider before they got to the jump. If he had a good jump, he'd try to hit the ground pedaling so he could pass the number five rider.

Then he would only have to stay in fifth place until the end, and he'd be in the semifinal for the first time. He hoped Mom and Dad and Jim and Maryann and Yolanda were all watching. He didn't have to hope, really. He knew they were cheering their heads off, too.

The sixth-place rider was harder to catch than Daniel thought. Daniel drew near him, and his front wheel came alongside. The other rider seemed more determined then ever. How Daniel wished he could take a deeper breath. Before the afternoon's competition, he would ask Dad and Jim to help him adjust that dumb strap.

For now he just held his breath—which wasn't a smart thing to do. He gritted his teeth as he tried to push past the next rider. He edged past as they went down the short hill. And Daniel had picked up such speed that he was almost even with the fifth place rider already.

He could hardly believe it. Rather than breathing, he just worked harder. He blasted up the jump and felt his bike fly way up in the air, higher than he had ever jumped before.

The only problem was, jumping so high wasn't good because it slowed him down. He got too much wind resistance. And the two riders he was closest to were able to stay closer to the ground. By the time he banged down hard onto the packed landing area, they had passed him again.

His breath burst from his lungs in a bark that surprised him. He had to fight to stay upright. He had gone into the air fast and had flown sideways. He had been able to straighten himself only a little before he landed.

His Malta XG wobbled crazily. He was panting as he saw the six riders ahead pulling away from him. His whole body ached now, and he wasn't sure he could catch them. But he had to! Today was the day he was at least going to make the semifinals.

Daniel had been in the A competition for only three weeks. It had been such a relief to be out of what he and his friends called "the baby class."

His father and brother had told him how important it was to learn slowly and completely before getting into the real competition. His dad reminded him that he would have been very discouraged if he had tried the top races first—and finished last in every one.

Now he knew his dad was right. But he had come a long way in just three short weeks of the better racing. He had never finished last, though he had been second to last. Three times he'd been in the top ten.

And now here he was in seventh with less than a half mile to go. He had been as high as tied for fifth. He figured if the fifth- and sixth-place riders were as tired as he was, he ought to be able to catch them both.

He put his head down and pedaled for all he was worth. The tight, slow turn was coming. He decided to take it faster than ever. He had nothing to lose.

2

Learning, Learning, Learning

Daniel grew more excited as he peeked behind and saw no one even coming over the rise yet. The riders in front of him seemed to relax a little after surviving the jump and before slowly maneuvering the tightest turn on the course.

He was panting. His tongue and throat were dry. He needed a break, some rest, something to drink. He needed to loosen his grip on the handlebars. He wanted to get his elbow and knee pads off and stretch out on his back. But not now.

Right now he had a job to do. He still had enough left for one more surge at the fifth- and sixth-place riders. He was just behind them, and they were closely trailing the leaders.

The course was flat. There were a few ruts before the turn. The whole group ahead of him, first through sixth, kept the distance between themselves as they all prepared for the turn. Daniel decided to make his move when they all sat down for the turn.

They had been standing, pushing, pumping, and driving. He was doing the same. He watched for the telltale sign of slowing. That would come when they quit pedaling. They would still be standing, ready to lean into the turn. And when they went around the curve, they would sit so they could put one foot out for balance if necessary.

Already there had been a slight slowdown. Daniel felt himself gaining on them. Almost as one, all six quit pedaling, preparing to lean and then sit. He pushed harder than ever.

As they all lowered themselves to their seats, Daniel flew past at top speed. He was still standing, still pushing as if he were on the straightaway. The fifth- and sixth-place riders looked up quickly, throwing themselves off stride.

Success! Daniel had passed them! If he could just stay there, but the curve was rushing toward him. The first four riders were into it. He had nowhere to go. He quickly dropped to his seat and stuck his left foot out. He leaned the bike way over in an attempt to stay on the track.

Daniel was going more than twice as fast as the other riders. He felt himself sliding into the turn. He could actually see his back tire out of the corner of his eye. He fought the handle bars to steer into his slide. And he sensed the leaders were reacting the same way the fifth- and sixth-place guys had.

They were surprised to see anyone join them, let alone pass them. And especially surprised to see Daniel's green jump suit. It wasn't a color they recognized as usually being that close to the lead this late in a race.

Daniel didn't know any of them personally. He had met a few of them before and between heats. He couldn't think about who they were just now, anyway. It was no longer a matter of just trying to maintain his fifth-place position for qualifying. He had to stay on the course and stay up, or he'd still be on the ground when the latecomers arrived.

He was shocked to find himself sliding out of control past the fourth-place rider and right next to the boy in third. The leaders were all coasting and leaning around the curve. They were getting ready to lift their balance feet and start pedaling again on the next straightaway.

Daniel was still pulling on the handlebar to keep the bike from flipping off the track. His left leg was dragging dustily on the ground. He felt the strain against his knee. His bike hit a deep rut at the outside of the curve. It hurled him past the leaders and directly in front of them as he headed for the old car tires marking the inside of the track.

All five riders directly behind him slammed on their brakes and skidded crazily. Somehow they avoided hitting him and each other. Daniel's bike rolled up and over one tire. His front wheel lodged inside another.

He stopped dead and almost flew off the front of his bike. He moaned in desperation as the other riders screamed and swore at him. "You jerk!" they yelled. "Learn to ride."

He yanked his bike from the old tire and jumped aboard. The first six riders were trying to get rolling again. From over the jump came the rest of the pack. Daniel didn't know whether to give up and let them pass him, or try to stay in the race, or what.

He was embarrassed that he had messed up the race for the leaders. But he was also excited that, even though he was way out of control and had done something foolish, he had—for an instant at least—been in the lead.

He liked the feeling. There had been no one ahead of him. Of course, there hadn't been any track ahead of him either. At the moment he was ahead and heading straight across the track toward the infield.

He boarded his bike again and tried to catch the leaders. He enjoyed for the mement the feeling that had come with being out ahead of everyone. *Someday I'm going to do that again,* he decided. *Only I'm going to be in control, not skidding. I'll be leading because I know what I'm doing.*

Even though he was more exhausted than ever, that thought made him want to at least hold his position and not embarrass himself even more. He knew it was too late to finish fifth. But he sure wanted to finish with the first pack.

He had run with his bike before jumping on. Somehow

that gave him an advantage over the leaders. They hadn't had to get off their bikes when they stopped; so they just started riding while still sitting on them. They probably should have jumped off and run before reboarding, the way Daniel had.

He found himself gaining on them again, just as they reached the hill. If he was going faster then they were, he'd have better luck on the hill. That made him stand up and dig even harder.

He had a million emotions in his mind. He had enjoyed the lead. But he knew it had been the result of foolishness rather than good riding. He had been embarrassed and humiliated by getting hung up in the tires. He had wanted just to finish respectably. But here he was gaining on the leaders again.

He knew he didn't have much stamina left. After the hill was a shallow downhill. Then there was a long straight and a big, sweeping curve. Everyone would take that at full speed before going into the short, final straightaway to the finish line.

Daniel decided that he would push himself as hard as he could up the hill. He could almost coast downhill. Then, if he was too tired, he'd just finish the best he could. If he could finish fifth, fine. If not, that was all right, too. He would have done the best he could. Even his bit of recklessness had shown him something new about himself.

He began pushing up the hill. The first thing he noticed was that the fourth-place rider was tiring quickly. He could hardly pedal enough to keep going. He was quickly passed by the fifth and sixth riders. And then by Daniel.

Daniel felt a little sorry for him. He recognized the uniform as the guy who had won the first heat before these quarter finals. Apparently, that had taken a lot out of him. But he would be a good bike racer someday when he developed more staying power. It was a demanding, exhausting sport. It made Daniel wonder how he himself would have anything left if he did qualify for the semifinals.

"Thanks a lot for throwing me off stride!" the other kid said as Daniel passed him.

"Sorry!" Daniel yelled. He really was, but he didn't expect the boy to believe him. He knew he'd not been wise. But he hadn't done it on purpose. When he did do it on purpose, maybe the following week, he'd do it better. He would pass everyone without messing them up.

Daniel's speed pushed him into fifth place. But the sixth-place rider didn't just let him by easily. He pushed him left and then right. Daniel really had to jump on the pedals to keep them moving fast enough. But that helped him up the hill, too.

He was so excited about having passed two riders and being in fifth place by the time he got to the top of the hill that he forgot about his weakness and his aching side and his thirst.

The other leaders were obviously going to try to take the long, wide turn at top speed. They would pick up as much as they could by still pedaling on their way downhill. Daniel wanted to coast. But who knew what the guy he just passed would do?

He kept standing and pedaling furiously. He couldn't believe the speed he was generating. In the first heat, he coasted down the hill and took the curve too carefully. Now he had already been through a treacherous curve. Luckily he didn't hurt himself or anyone else. This one should be easy.

3

The Complaint

Daniel felt the cramps in his legs as he wheeled down the hill. He seemed to be gaining a little more on the leaders. As they leaned into the turn, still standing and pedaling hard, he did the same.

They peeked back as they all entered the straightaway. He was just behind fourth place and well ahead of the sixth-place rider. It felt good. Real good. Almost too good. He would qualify for the semifinals for the first time. He could even picture himself getting one of the first three prizes—the trophy for first, or one of the ribbons for second and third.

But he had nothing more left for this quarter final. He was spent. Worn out. He sat down and quit pedaling. The first four pulled away from him, fighting each other for the lead. They weren't content just to qualify for the next race. They wanted great times. They wanted to win the heat.

He looked back. The sixth-place rider was gaining on him. But Daniel knew he had enough of a lead to coast in ahead of him. Daniel finished fifth by about two feet. The first four were doing wheelies and showing off and raising their fists.

All Daniel could do was sit and let both feet drag on either side. He slowly removed himself from the Malta XG. He let it rest against his thigh as he pulled off his gloves and unsnapped his helmet. He also unsnapped the button at the neck of his jumpsuit and took a deep breath.

He didn't know which felt better, to be finished or to have qualified.

The announcer said, "The last quarter final will begin in ten minutes." Daniel wanted to watch it. He wanted to see Randy in action again. But now he just wanted to find his family and stretch out awhile.

With his gloves in his helmet and his helmet under one arm, he walked his bike to the edge of the track. He began looking for the blanket where his family would be waiting. They used to sit in the stands. Then they found they could see just as much and enjoy the long day of racing even more if they could eat and sit on the ground.

Now they were standing, waving, and clapping as he caught sight of them. He felt good. *What a family!* he thought. Many of the other riders didn't have families. Or if they did, they only showed up once in a while.

Then there were the other kinds of families, the kinds who hassled their kids if they lost. Daniel had a feeling that that was the kind of family Randy Hickock had. His parents and two teenage brothers came to every race, along with his little sister. They never had to even talk with him about losing, of course. But they were always yelling at the officials and carrying on about violations and incorrect timing and all that. Daniel wondered what they would do if Randy ever lost a race.

I wouldn't mind causing that someday, he thought. But not today.

His mother was waving and pointing to a thermos of lemonade. That looked like gold to him right then. But as he started toward his family, he felt a large hand on his shoulder.

"Son," an official said, "are you number fifteen?"

"Yes, sir."

"There's been a complaint lodged against you. Could you come with me?"

"What do you mean?"

"One of the other riders has charged you with a foul on the tight turn. He feels you willfully impeded his progress."

"What does that mean?"

"Got in his way on purpose and kept him from going ahead."

"I didn't! I just got going too fast and got out of control! I didn't hit anybody and nobody hit me. And I sure didn't mean to do it. I thought that was the rule. That unless you hit somebody on purpose, you were all right."

"That is the rule, son. And if the corner judge saw it the way you see it, there'll be no problem. If he agrees with the complaint, though, you change positions with the other rider."

"What place did he finish?"

"Seventh."

"You mean he would qualify, and I wouldn't?"

"You finished fifth, didn't you?"

Daniel nodded.

"Then that's right. You would be out of the running. He would be in fifth. You can leave your bike with someone if you'd like."

By now, Jim had come to the edge of the track, wondering what was going on. "Can you take my bike for a minute, Jim?" Daniel asked. He told him about the charge.

"Hey," Jim shouted. "That's not right! I saw it! Daniel didn't hit anyone, and no one hit him. And the guy who dropped back just ran out of steam going up the hill!"

"Jim!" Daniel said. "Let me argue for myself, OK?"

Jim looked a little sheepish. Daniel was embarrassed. He didn't want his family acting just like Randy Hickock's. He followed the official to the scoring table in the infield. The other rider was there, and so was the corner judge.

"Daniel," the corner judge said, "I'm Frank O'Neal. Do you know this other rider?"

Daniel shook his head, finding it hard not to glare at the boy, who was also alone.

"Well," the judge said. "His name is Tom Engle. And he's lodged a complaint against you."

"I know, but I. . ."

"Now, Mr. Bradford, if you don't mind, I'd like to be in charge of this. This is a learning experience for both of you, and our goal is good sportsmanship. That's what dirt bike racing is all about in this county. I'd like both of you to see how we do this. And I want to get it done quickly enough that one of you can compete in the semifinals."

"I'd like to watch the next quarter final," Daniel said.

"Maybe," the judge said. "Tom has already told his side of the story. Would you like to tell yours?"

"You mean I don't get to hear what he said?"

"We could have him repeat it if you want to take the time, Daniel."

"No, I think I can guess. I'm sure he said I got in his way." The judge nodded. "Well, I did, but I didn't do it on purpose. I'm kind of new at this. I was trying my best to qualify. So when I thought everyone would be slowing down for that curve, I decided to try to speed through it. I almost made it. In fact, I got ahead of everyone. But then I couldn't really make the curve right. I hit that rut, and it threw me onto the inside of the track and into the tires. But I didn't hit anybody, and nobody hit me. And when I started again, Tom here was in second or third place. He slowed down after I started up the hill."

Tom Engle was shaking his head.

"I'm sorry, Tom," the judge said, "but that's just the way I saw it. Daniel did not use the best judgment. But I don't feel he impeded anyone's progress on purpose. And I also feel that all of the others he got in front of had the same disadvantage. He wound up passing only two of you. Yourself as you slowed down going up the hill, and another by his own riding skill. Daniel stays in fifth, and you stay in seventh.

"Now boys, I hope you both learned something from this process. Tom, you should always feel free to lodge a complaint. Daniel, you will always get your say. And Daniel, I hope, too, that you learned something about careful riding today."

"I did. I know if I try to take a curve that fast again, I should be prepared."

The judge smiled. "I'd like you two to shake hands. And I think it would be good if you got to know each other better and maybe became friends."

Daniel thrust out his hand.

"Forget it!" Tom snarled. His light brown hair blew in the wind as his dark eyes flashed. "That's no fair! I always qualify for the semifinals. Just wait till we're in the same race again, Bradford! You'll wish you never got into this sport!"

"Now, Tom," the judge said. "Let's not have any of that."

But Tom hurried away. The judge shrugged apologetically to Daniel. "He's upset," he said. "But don't worry about future races with him. I'll be watching out for you."

"Thanks."

Daniel's family was eager to hear all about the protest. They were even more excited to know that Daniel would be in the semifinals.

"I want to talk some strategy with you," Jim said. "If you don't mind."

Daniel lay down on the blanket and sipped some lemonade. "I don't mind," he said.

"I think you could have won that heat."

"Now that I mind," Daniel said, sitting up. "You have no idea how much it took out of me to finish fifth. I'm not sure I can even handle the semifinal."

"Dan," his father said. "I agree with Jim. I know you tried hard. And I saw what you tried to do in that corner. But you could have won it."

"You said you didn't care if I ever won as long as I

enjoyed racing!" Daniel said. "Now you're pushing me. Just because you want to brag about me or something."

"That's not it at all," his father said sternly. "Now do you want to hear our side of it or not?"

"I guess."

"I'm not going to talk about it if you think I'm pushing you or am disappointed in you. Because I'm not. I'm proud of you."

"It's all right. You can."

"But first let's watch the other quarter final. Then we've got to get your bike in shape for the semi's."

Yolanda and Maryann were already working on the bike. They cleaned the dirt and dust from the chain and wheels and wiped down the rest of it.

"I'll check all the nuts and bolts in a while," Jim said. "So you can qualify for the finals."

Daniel dropped down on his back again and sighed. It was going to be a long day.

4
Randy's Show

Daniel actually dozed for about five minutes before the announcement of the other quarter final race.

As soon as it was announced, even before he could get his eyes opened and accustomed to the light, Dad and Jim were signaling him to follow them. They went over to the fence where they could see the entire race course at one time.

"I want you just to watch this Hickock kid," his dad said.

"Dad, I've seen him a million times. I mean, I want to see him, too, but I don't think there's anything he does that I haven't seen."

"There might be a few things you missed, Dan, that's all," Jim said. "Let's study him. You know why?"

"No, why?"

"Because even though he's a year older than you are, he's no bigger. And he shouldn't be any stronger. Somehow his feet move faster. He seems to have more power. He may have a lighter, tougher bike, but that doesn't account for his ability to beat you by forty seconds in a one-mile qualifier."

"I've never raced against him," Daniel said defensively.

"Yeah, but today you could get your chance. I'm comparing your best time with his. He must be doing something right. Will he goof around and be a hot dog in this race?"

"Probably not," Daniel said. "There are some pretty good riders in this heat. He'll win. But he probably won't be able to mess around."

"Then it'll be a perfect one to study," Mr. Bradford said.

"Do you want me to be as good as Randy?" Daniel asked.

His dad threw his arm around him. "I just want you to be as good as you can be, Dan. If there are good things he's doing that you can apply to your own riding, then you'll want to do it so you'll enjoy it more. Right?"

"I guess. I thought you just wanted me to have a good time."

"Won't you have a better time if you do better and win once in a while?"

"I suppose."

"How about if you beat Randy someday?"

"That'll be the day!"

"Well, would you like it or not? Or have you already given up on that?"

Daniel shook his head. "I don't know."

"Well, let's watch," Jim said.

The riders lined up in four rows of five each. Randy Hickock was in the middle of the first row. When the gun sounded, Randy shot into the lead. He was ahead by ten feet by the time he got to the dip before the jump.

"Look at that," Jim said. "Did you notice how relaxed he is? Everyone else is gripping the handlebars like they're trying to choke them to death. He has a very light touch. His legs are going a mile a minute, sure. But the bike is wobbling back and forth so he can put the most pressure possible on each pedal. Look at that! He just adjusted his helmet with one hand. He didn't slow down or swerve at all!"

Daniel was amazed. Randy was so much better than anyone else that he had almost beaten them already. As he flew over the jump, he stayed low. Somehow he didn't even have to adjust his flight. He hit the ground straight and pedaling. Everyone behind him flew high and bounced as they landed, having to fight to keep their balance.

They all were trying to stay upright. Randy was standing, staring ahead, and keeping his bike perfectly straight.

"He's choosing a higher line!" Jim shouted. "Look at him avoid the ruts and take a straight shot at the corner."

Amazingly, Randy approached the corner the same way Daniel had. But rather than sliding through it and winding up almost in the infield, he jumped on the brake at the last instant. Still standing he slid around the corner and started pedaling as he hit the straightaway.

Up the hill he still had stamina. He was actually pulling away from the rest of the pack even more. And they were still on flat ground. All eyes were on him as he reached the top and raced down the other side. He was going so fast when he went around the big, sweeping curve that Daniel thought sure he would wipe out.

But Randy was steady. He was flying at top speed. He never wavered, never slowed down. To stay steady at one point, he raised his body up rather than staying in a crouch. That let the wind slow him enough to keep him on the track.

"Wow!" Jim shouted. "Did you see that?" It made Daniel a little jealous. He was learning one thing though. He would probably never be able to race as fast or as well as Randy Hickock. Randy's time was going to be faster than the next older age group. And it wouldn't bother Daniel at all if they moved Randy up a class—or even two! *If I never had to race against him,* he thought, *it would be all right with me.*

When Randy came around for his second lap, he did everything precisely the same way he had the first time. Exactly. Top speed, bike straight, approaching the tight curve full bore, sliding around it, charging up the hill.

Then he changed. When he got to the top, he quit pedaling and sat down. He looked behind him just before he went down the other side. There were only two others riders in sight. They were fighting each other for second place. Neither had a chance at catching him.

So he coasted. He just sat there, feet still, head bent over the handlebars. He let gravity pull him down the hill and around the curve. As he got to the straightaway, he was going very slowly, but the second- and third-place riders were just coming over the hill.

Randy had to pedal a little to stay upright on the last straightaway. But he coasted past the finish line with plenty of room to spare. The reaction from the crowd was a combination of cheers and boos. His time going into the second lap was ahead of the course record—not only for his and Daniel's age group, but for the next age group as well.

It was obvious that Randy was saving all his strength for the semifinal and final.

"I hope I'm not in his semi," Daniel said. "That automatically takes away one of my chances of qualifying. I don't think I've got enough left to qualify anyway."

"That's what we need to talk about," Mr. Bradford said. "Attitude."

"Oh, Dad! My attitude's fine! I'm just being realistic."

"You want to get away from here over lunch? The semifinals aren't till one o'clock. You and Jim and I could go for hamburgers and talk."

"How do you think Mom and the girls will feel about that? Didn't Mom pack a picnic?"

"Yeah, but they can have the picnic. We need to talk."

Daniel shrugged. When they got back to the rest of the family, Mr. and Mrs Bradford talked privately. Daniel's mother seemed to agree. But when she suggested the plan to Maryann and Yolanda, they were upset.

"No fair!" Yolanda. "Let us go and you stay here!"

"Yeah!" Maryann chimed in, smiling. "You can't argue with that."

"That doesn't get Daniel away from here for a while," Jim said.

"Who said I wanted to get away! I didn't say that. Let's stay. I just want to rest."

But when his mother and two sisters drove off to the hamburger place, Daniel wished he'd gone with them. He knew that he was going to get the same old lecture from his dad and Jim. And he was right. But he also got something he didn't bargain for.

5

The Encounter

Daniel felt a little embarrased when his father asked Jim to pray before they ate. Jim didn't make it a loud or long, drawn-out affair. So Daniel wasn't uncomfortable for too long. He wanted to ask his father if praying in public wasn't the very thing that Jesus criticized the religious leaders of His day for doing.

But he had heard that lecture before, too. And he knew his father had a point. You don't do it for show, he had always said. But you don't change your private habits in public just for the sake of your own comfort. Those few people who do notice are sometimes favorably impressed by others praying before a meal.

Daniel ate in silence. Jim and Mr. Bradford talked with each other about how impressive Randy had been.

Finally, Daniel interrupted. "Do you know that no one can stand him?"

"Oh, that doesn't surprise me," Mr. Bradford said. "People are always jealous of the top banana."

"Yeah, but no one was unhappy about the guy who won my quarter final. He's a nice kid. He's a good, fair racer. And he gives it all he's got. I was happy for him. He was the best in our group. Nobody's mad at him or thinks he's a creep."

"And they do with the Hickock boy?"

"Sure they do! Look at how he hot dogged it when he had that big lead, Dad. I don't even think he did the wrong thing. He slowed down and saved himself for the next two races. He doesn't have to go for the record every time. But to turn around and look, and shrug, and just coast like that. He was showing off. Nobody likes that."

Daniel's dad nodded slowly, as if he was thinking deeply. "Good point, Dan," he said. "Very good point. And what about you, when you passed enough people to qualify? Did you let up?"

"Yeah, but. . ."

"Yeah, but nothing, Dan," Jim interrupted. "You let up. Maybe you weren't showing off, and maybe you're no Randy Hickock yet, but you did just enough to qualify and nothing more."

"I don't believe you guys," Daniel said. "You weren't out there. You don't know what I went through. I made a lot of mistakes. My chin strap was so tight I could hardly breathe. So a couple of times I held my breath. Smart, huh? Really stupid! And that happened right when I made my biggest mistake."

"Mistake?" Jim said. "What do you consider a mistake? Until you quit, you rode a very nice race."

"Are you kiddng? I took that tight turn so fast on the second lap that there was no way I could handle it. I was lucky I had a few feet on those guys before the rut threw me in front of them. I could have knocked over six guys!"

"But, Daniel!" Mr. Bradford said. "Don't you see that that was great? You weren't trying to knock anybody over. You were just trying to do your best. It would have been horrible if you'd hit anyone or caused anyone to fall. But your idea was right! Randy Hickock, if he been in sixth or seventh place there, would have done the same thing. He wouldn't have flown into the infield, of course. But he would have tried to take advantage of everyone else's being careful. I was so proud of you!"

"You were? Really?"

His father nodded.

"So was I," Jim said. "And we could tell you were tired. And that you were working harder than you ever had before. When you went charging up that hill, we thought you were going after the lead. You can imagine how disappointed we were when you looked around, saw you had fifth place locked up, and quit."

"I couldn't have won that heat! It was all I could do to get into fifth. That's not bad for the short time I've been racing. This is the only track I've ever raced on. You know Randy has raced on more than a hundred courses? He's even been on television."

"Everybody in California gets on TV sometime," Jim muttered.

"We're not saying you didn't do an outstanding job, Dan," his father said. "And maybe you didn't have anything left after your super effort. But it really looked like you let up."

"I don't think I had a choice. There was nothing left."

"Maybe, Dan. Maybe you're right. But tell me this: if you'd been in sixth place and you saw the fifth-place guy slowing some, what would you have done?"

Daniel had to think about that one for a while.

"I'm sure glad that wasn't what happened," he said. "I don't know where I would have got the extra strength. But—"

"You would have gone after him, wouldn't you?"

"Yeah, I guess I would have."

"Then I want to see you go after the leaders the same way. You did a fantastic thing. You showed yourself you can compete with the best racers here."

"Except Randy."

"Maybe. But you led that heat for a few seconds. Then you had those guys in your sights. And I'll always believe you could have chased them down. Maybe you couldn't have beat them, but you could have given the first two a run for their money. Think so?"

"Maybe. But I wouldn't have got anything for it. First through fifth qualified for the semifinals. So it didn't make any difference."

"How can you say that, Dan?" Jim said. "Besides the reward of knowing you did your best, there are some practical reasons for finishing first in the quarter finals."

"Like what."

"First, you score overall points. It gives you a higher rating. That puts you in easier qualifying heats later. And the better you do in your qualifiers, the fewer times you have to face Randy until the final. I'll bet you face him in the semi's because you were one of the slowest qualifiers. They put the fastest with the slowest so the finals will have the absolute fastest riders."

"Hm," Daniel said.

"Besides that," Mr. Bradford said, "there's a reason to want to do your best all the time. Unless you're saving yourself for a more important race."

"I know," Daniel said. "Because the Bible says God wants us to do everything heartily as unto the Lord."

"Do you take that seriously?"

Daniel shrugged. "I do for important stuff."

"Like what?"

"Like schoolwork. And trying to obey you and Mom."

"This is important, too, Dan."

"Why? Because you'll be embarrassed if I don't do well?"

"That's not it at all, Dan. I've told you and told you that I just want you to have fun and enjoy it. I don't want to put pressure on you to do better than you're able. But if you're going to do something, it's worth doing right. We have a lot of money tied up in this sport. You know this dirt bike cost as much as your ten-speed because you helped pay for it. And your uniform cost that much more again. Then there's insurance and entry fees."

"I know."

"But I'm more than happy to do it, Dan. If you enjoy it and like it and look forward to it."

"And if I'm great?"

"No. If you do your best. That's all. It's good practice for the really important things in life. If you do everything the best you can, you'll know you gave it all you had—whether you're the best or the worst compared to everyone else."

Two boys approached. Daniel recognized them immediately.

"Hi, Randy," he said. "Hi, Tom."

Daniel introduced his father and brother to the two boys. "That was some race we just saw, Randy," Mr. Bradford said.

"Yeah," Jim chimed in.

"Thanks," Randy said. "Actually, it was a piece of cake. This age category is boring for me, you know."

"Yes," Mr. Bradford said, suddenly getting serious. "You made the end of the race a little boring, too."

Randy raised his eyebrows. "I was just trying to make it more interesting. Hard to do without better competition."

Daniel decided to be bold. "You ready to shake hands yet, Tom? You know I didn't mean to mess up your race. And I don't really think I caused you to lose."

Tom reached for Daniel's hand. "Yeah, well, you can think what you want. But what I said earlier still stands. I'll look forward to next week."

"And I'll look forward to one o'clock," Randy said. "I like to get a look at who I'm competing against. Even if you did only just qualify in fifth place, I saw your move in the corner there. Pretty impressive. I'll know enough to be way ahead of you before then."

"It was an accident," Daniel said. "I thought I was a better rider than I am."

"Yeah, sure," Randy said. "That was as much an accident as my winning that last race."

6

The Start

Daniel's mother and two sisters arrived back at the race-track park a few minutes before the two semifinal races began. Daniel was in the first heat, along with Randy Hickock and eighteen other riders. Only the first five from each semifinal would ride in the finals for trophies and ribbons.

Daniel watched the end of the junior girls' race. He wondered whether Yolanda might want to try racing someday. She had shown no interest so far. But maybe he could talk her into it. He was sure she would like it.

A lot of things went through Daniel's mind as he walked his bike through the gate at the far end of the track. Slowly he began preparing for his race. He carefully laid his bike on its side—racing dirt bikes have no kickstands—and snapped his jump suit up to the neck.

Then he put on his helmet. It was heavy and hot. But even though he hated wearing it, he knew he was safer in it. He pulled his gloves on slowly. He yanked them up toward his wrists as far as he could. He wrapped the strips around and zipped the cuffs on his sleeves.

He felt a little like a space man. But he was ready. He

breathed deeply. He thought of all the things his dad and brother had said over lunch. He didn't know why he had given them such a hard time.

He felt they were pushing him more than he wanted to be pushed. But on the other hand, Daniel believed him when Dad said he just wanted Daniel to do his best. And of course, they were right about doing your best if you're going to do something at all.

As much as Daniel said otherwise, he knew that one of the reasons for bike racing in the first place was to see how well he could do at it. It always looked like so much fun on television. A person couldn't make a whole life out of it, but it could be great for a while.

He wanted to become good, very good. He wasn't doing it just for fun. He wanted to excel at something. He'd always been a fair basketball player and an average baseball player. But this year he was giving up baseball after three years in Little League. He wanted to be better than average.

Other kids had been in bike racing since they were five or six. But he knew he'd catch on. He'd always been pretty good on his ten-speed. In fact, he didn't know anyone who could beat him in a straight race on that bike.

When he first told his parents about the bike races, they came to see a few. They decided that if he really wanted to get into it, they'd help him. If he paid for half the bike, they would pay for all the equipment and other costs. He thought that was a good idea.

He mowed lawns and did odd jobs in the neighborhood to help pay off his half of the bike. It wasn't that his parents couldn't afford it without his help. Of course they could. But they wanted to help him learn responsibility and to have a sense of ownership in the bike. And Daniel liked the feeling of earning something.

He had taken good care of it. He studied a lot of books. He listened when older riders told him how to keep the bike oiled and clean and in good shape. And he rode it every day. Some days he would go for distance, riding ten miles at a good pace. Other days, he would ride a course that took him up and down hills and around tight curves. Then one day a week he rode the bike as hard as he could over rugged terrain. He fell frequently, even though he forced himself to try to keep his balance over the rough spots.

He loved it. He had jumped from beginners' to class A in three weeks of racing. Now, three weeks later, he was in his first semifinal. He didn't want to sound negative. But he was pretty sure he was not among the top five racers in this semi. In fact, he knew he had the second slowest qualifying time of all twenty racers in the race.

But he had stopped dead on the track at one point. And he hadn't had the best start. His quarter final hadn't had the advantage of having Randy Hickock leading the way either. A rider like Randy pulled everyone else to faster times than they had ever ridden before.

By the time Daniel got to the starting area, he had talked himself into the race. He had been tired, but he had also had a good rest. And he had not been injured or anything. He was healthy, active, in shape, and eleven years old. He should be able to ride this race as fast as possible without hurting himself.

He still hadn't learned to breathe too well while riding. But that would come. And his father had loosened his chin strap. Now he could breathe while still keeping his helmet secure.

Daniel just wished that the local rules allowed the racers to start by running alongside their bikes and jumping on when they wanted to. That would take care of a lot of the early spills. The faster runners would be farther ahead and out of all the traffic. He would have been one of the faster runners. He didn't know whether Randy would. Randy didn't look fast or slow. He just couldn't tell.

A rider could run and jump on if he fell on the course. That was to protect him from getting run over. It also helped him get back into the race quickly.

But at the start, everyone had to have one foot on the

ground. The other was on whichever pedal he chose. Daniel was surprised at the number of riders who started with their pedal foot down and the other on the ground. When the gun sounded, they stepped up to the high pedal. Daniel thought they lost a good second or two trying to get going.

He put his right foot on the pedal. He had the pedal at the top of the sprocket and his left foot on the ground. Then, when the gun sounded, he simply shifted all his weight to his right foot, straightened the bike up, and let his weight give him the send-off.

He was placed second to the outside of the last row. That was the second to the worst position. From where he stood, though, he could see Randy in the front row, getting ready for the gun. He stood poised just as Daniel did. *At least I'm doing something right,* Daniel decided. If only that were all there was to it.

There was a lot of jockeying for position, especially with the riders in the back rows. Their job was to get to the inside as quickly as possible. They had to get ahead of as many riders as they could. If they couldn't overcome the handicap of where they started, the first row would qualify for the finals and that would be the end of it.

As it was, the first row was made up of the riders with the five fastest times in two quarter final races.

Daniel decided on his strategy. He would maintain his position, even letting the outside rider get inside him. Everyone else was inside him or ahead of him anyway. He would let them all fight among themselves on the inside. That way he would have a straighter shot at the front group.

The leaders would bunch up along the inside, too. So he should have the middle to the outside of the track pretty much to himself. He would take the first straightaway and the jump and the tight curve right there. Then he would try to pass any of the slower riders he could on the way up the steep hill.

His first big move would be on the downside of the hill and the long curve. He assumed everyone had figured out that that was where a lot of time could be made up. But he had learned how to navigate that turn from watching Randy do it.

Everyone went unbelievably fast down the hill. But they slowed some going into the turn. Randy wouldn't. And neither would Daniel. He wasn't sure he could pull off that trick of straightening up and letting the wind slow him down a little. But it was worth a try.

He wasn't expected to qualify anyway. So what did he have to lose? His boldness had paid off in the quarter final. So he was ready to try a little more this time.

His breathing came shallow and short. He was excited. He didn't want to be out of breath before the gun. But he was so ready and determined that he couldn't help it. The officials took their time clearing out of the way.

Now it was just riders and bikes and the starter.

Everyone was still except the rider next to Daniel and one in the third row. They were still moving around to get just the right comfortable stance and feeling before the gun sounded.

"Riders to your marks!" the starter barked, raising his blank pistol.

"Set!"

Blam!

7

The Battle

There was one thing Daniel had not reminded himself of. And he didn't think of it until the race was underway. That was that he should relax at the start the way Randy Hickock always did. Daniel found himself squeezing the handlebar grips so tightly that his fingers almost locked into position.

The rider to his right was surprised when Daniel let him pass to get to the inside. Soon the race course was just the way Daniel had planned it. He was to the right of the middle of the track on high, smooth dirt. All nineteen other riders were tight to the inside in one or two lines. They were trying to ride the shortest distance they could before they reached the jump, the tight curve, and the steep climb.

He couldn't really see Randy. But he knew Randy would be way out ahead already. There were a couple of riders who might stay fairly close to him until the hill. But they would soon fall back behind him.

Daniel's racing plan had one problem. Even though he was all alone and had clear sailing, he was not yet going as fast as everyone else. He wasn't really even in the race at all.

He was riding well, and he was moving quickly, but he was dead last.

As he approached the jump, no one else was in sight. They had all flown down to the other side and were approaching the tight turn. He decided he'd better get going if he was going to have any chance of competing. Unfortunately, he already felt tired. He had never ridden this many races in one day before.

Daniel shot down the dip and went up over the rise. He tried to stay low so he wouldn't lose too much time. Then, while he was in the air, he saw it. A mess. A pile of bikes and riders, at least a dozen of them.

Someone had fallen going around the turn and had caused a chain reaction of flying bikes and bodies. As he swept around them on the outside, he noticed that no one looked hurt. All were trying to untangle themselves and get back on their bikes.

The thought of having more than half the competition hung up at the curve gave Daniel a surge of energy. He could go around that curve the same way he had in the quarter finals. He knew that his momentum would carry him into the rut that would throw him toward the infield. When it happened, he decided, he would just fight to keep from hitting the tires and keep going toward the hill.

He blasted toward the curve at full speed, still standing. He wasn't even going to hit the brakes at the last instant the way Randy did. That was probably the better way to do it. But he had never tried it and would have to work hard to keep the bike under control.

He raced past all the bikes on the ground as fast as he could. He went into the turn without slowing down even the slightest. Then he merely quit pumping as he felt the bike going into the slide. He fought the skid, turned back toward the slide, and kept coasting. He felt himself driven from the rut toward the inside just as he had before. Only this time, no one was in his way. The fallen riders—later he would learn that fourteen had gone down—were just getting back on their bikes. And the five riders ahead of him were already on their way up the hill.

He was thrown across the track. He wobbled terribly as he narrowly missed the tires. He had to wonder whether anyone, even Randy, had ever gone around that turn at that speed without falling or crashing into the tires. He doubted it.

Soon his bike was straight again. And he began pedaling hard. He had come off the curve with such unusual speed that he started to the hill before the others had reached the top. Again, he was gaining on them. And to his amazement, the rider closest to him was Randy!

What was Randy doing in fifth place? Was he playing a game? Had he decided just to barely qualify and save his best racing for the final? No, that didn't sound like him. He might be teasing the other riders, but he would win, certainly. He had never lost, as Daniel knew.

Maybe he had been involved in the mess at the curve. Maybe he had had the lead and then slowed way down, making the others crash behind him. Maybe someone decided to stay right with him at the beginning and he had to be really skillful to make it through the curve.

Maybe he almost fell and was in fifth place now because the others were truly challenging him. Daniel just didn't know. He did know that if he was there for the picking, Daniel wanted a shot at him.

He drove hard up the hill. He lost sight of the leaders as they went down the other side. Already, Randy was starting to make his move. Whatever had happened at the start, he was finished running fifth. Daniel knew what Randy was up to.

Randy moved to the inside. He began picking up speed. Daniel was about twenty five feet behind him and followed right in his tracks. As the lead riders moved into the wide turn, they slowed down and stayed near the middle of the track.

Daniel could hardly believe Randy's plan. But it was

clear he was going to take that curve as he normally did. He would let his momentum carry him high to the outside, no matter who was in the way. And there were four there.

Daniel faced a decision. He knew what Randy was going to do. Should he do the same? Why not? Randy's speed would carry him right past the others. And his angle toward the outside would force them the same way or make them slow down.

Daniel realized quickly that he was going every bit as fast as Randy. Maybe he was going faster because he had gone up the hill without having slowed down around the tight curve. While he was deciding, he maintained his speed. Soon, he had no choice.

He was going so fast and was so committed to doing whatever Randy did that it was too late to change his mind. Randy breezed past the front four. Daniel noticed them all hesitate as Randy charged up toward the fence and barreled around that curve onto the long straightaway.

Daniel was certain Randy had regained the lead for good. And he could tell the others felt the same. What they didn't know, however, was that Daniel was about to pass them at the same speed Randy had.

They were just settling back down from the higher part of the track as Daniel rocketed by. He made them move out a little more as they saw him out of the corners of their eyes. Daniel was thrilled over being in second place and leaving the former front-runners way behind him.

Somehow Randy was pulling away. But that didn't bother Daniel. He knew he was easily going to qualify for the finals, and that was good enough. He had not expected to beat Randy. In fact, he had not expected to qualify.

There was one more half-mile lap to go, but he knew he could handle it. He glanced over his shoulder. The third-through the sixth-place riders—the ones he and Randy had just blown past—were now having to fight off the rest of the pack.

Ahead of him, Randy was impressive. He was still at

top speed, but he looked relaxed. He was maintaining that incredibly straight line. He was using absolutely as little of the course as necessary. It was, as Jim had once remarked, "as if he's actually riding a shorter distance than everyone else, besides being faster."

Daniel knew he could do no better than to try to imitate Randy during the second lap. Even if one or two others caught him, he would still qualify. But then he remembered what his father and brother had said. *Don't get comfortable. Don't settle for just qualifying and saving yourself. Do your best, no matter what.*

They actually thought he could have won his quarter final. He didn't, but the more he thought about it, he wondered. What if he had reached down for that last little bit? What if he had pretended he was in sixth instead of in fifth?

He wondered what it would be like to pretend that he was in sixth place now, and that Randy was in fifth instead of leading. Stranger things had happened. He had seen Randy in fifth place in this very race. Maybe it was a fluke. Maybe something had happened. But maybe it had been Randy's fault. Maybe it was a mistake he could make again.

Maybe it was a mistake Randy could be rattled into if he was challenged this late in the race. He'd certainly be surprised if little ol' beginner Daniel Bradford pulled up near him in the tight curve, wouldn't he?

8

Bad Sport

Daniel knew his family had to be going nuts, watching him challenge Randy Hickock. Second place! Who would have believed it?

He knew exactly what Randy would do at the tight curve. The same thing he did every time. Go into it standing and pumping. Then brake to slide around it at the last instant. Daniel peeked behind him. No one was close.

What he would do, he decided, was to do the same thing he did the first time, too. He would still be trailing Randy, so he wouldn't shoot across in front of him. And there was no one close enough behind him to hinder, either. Then, if he had the speed he hoped he had, he might be able to catch Randy going up the hill.

He had proved the first time around that he could ride that long curve the same way Randy did. So if he could only get near him, catch him soon, he might actually be able to beat him at his own game.

Daniel had no thought about breaking any records. He knew the slowdown on the first lap had eliminated that possibility. Randy's experience and speed and maybe even better bike might carry him past Daniel for the victory. But it would still be the best race anyone had had against Randy since he showed up from California.

Daniel was so excited just thinking about it that he went into the tight curve faster than ever. In the next split second, though, he understood what had caused the accident on the first lap. It came to him in a flash.

Randy had tried Daniel's technique. Apparently, he had almost succeeded, because he hadn't fallen. He must have been in the lead when he shot across everyone else's path, causing the pileup. Maybe he'd had to stop and restart. Maybe that's the reason he was in fifth place when Daniel caught him.

Daniel knew that must have been what had happened, because Randy tried it again. Only this time, the rut didn't throw Randy in front of anyone.

Daniel, having made the turn that way more times, did it better and faster. And when Randy had to put both feet down to keep from hitting the tires in the infield, Daniel smashed into his back tire. That sent both bikes and both riders tumbling to the dirt.

Randy jumped up screaming and swearing. His handlebar was caught in Daniel's front wheel. But instead of waiting for Daniel to help him remove it, he just wrenched it free. He stomped on Daniel's bike several times while he did it.

He kept looking over his shoulder for the other riders. Daniel limped to his own bike. He quickly moved to the infield to get back on so he wouldn't be in the way of the other riders. Randy, though, put his bike right in the middle of the track and ran alongside it. He hopped on just as several other riders caught him.

They were all going faster than Randy, of course, but Randy was still ahead by a few feet. He rode back and forth in front of them, forcing them to slow down or swerve.

By the time he started up the hill, he at least matched their speed, had the lead, and blasted off from there. He was not relaxed anymore.

He was mad, rigid, fierce, and gripping the handlebars just as everyone else was.

Daniel wanted to get back in the race, but he was amazed by the fact that he was in last place again, just like that. Apparently all those bikers who had fallen on the first lap had had time to make up some ground on everyone except him and Randy. When there was a second accident, they all caught up.

Now following Randy was a tightly bunched group of riders, all fighting for the four qualifying places after him. And Daniel's front tire rim was bent.

As he moved back out onto the track, he noticed it wasn't rolling correctly. His father had always told him that if anything was wrong with the bike, never try to get back in a race. It was too dangerous—and too risky for the bike, too.

Daniel wanted to cry. He had learned so much about the course, and racing, and Randy. He thought he could have qualified for the finals. No, he still didn't think he was ready to beat Randy. But to make the finals the same week he reached his first semifinal would have been fantastic!

He pulled the Malta XG back into the infield and up over the rise where he could see the rest of the race. An official ran to him.

"You OK, son?"

"Yeah, I think so."

"How about your bike?"

"It's going to need a little work, but it's all right."

"I didn't see any foul. All fair-and-square as far as I could see. Not your fault."

"Thanks. But he'll probably file a protest anyway," Daniel said.

The man nodded toward the leader. "Shouldn't need to. Why protest when you win?"

Indeed, Randy was flying ahead of everyone else. He was into his patented wide sweep around the long curve and was pulling away. When he got to the straightaway, he raised one fist and roared past the finish line. Then he put both hands down and pulled his bike up into a wheelie.

There wasn't the usual cheering. And Randy was so intense that he pushed too hard with his feet and pulled too hard with his hands. Going almost full speed into a wheelie, he pulled the bike over backwards and flopped in the dirt.

At first, he looked as if he was going to try to act as if he had done it on purpose. He almost kept his feet. But then he lost the bike. It rolled end over end into the fence. And he rolled on the track, his helmet coming half off.

Officials and other bikers came running from everywhere to see whether he was all right. But as Daniel's father often said, nothing was hurt but his pride.

The rest of the finishers had to swerve around the fallen winner. But he quickly dusted himself off, got his bike, and headed for his own family. Daniel watched from his perch on the rise. And just as Randy got off the track and through the gate, Randy turned back and looked all around.

He spotted Daniel and started at him, his helmet under his arm. Daniel just stared right back, thinking about making some sort of gesture of apology. Then he realized that he had done nothing wrong.

Randy pointed at him and drew his finger across his neck. It was a threat. It meant, "Next time, watch out."

Daniel decided that he would be back next week—if he could get his bike repaired in time. And he would take brother Jim up on his offer to help train him and have him in even better shape.

Daniel didn't respond to Randy's threat. He just sat down next to his bike to rest and look over the damage. And to wait for the protest, if Randy was low enough to file one. Sure enough, he was.

Randy came by with his father a few minutes later. He didn't even look at Daniel. Soon an official came for him. He didn't say anything. He just beckoned him with one finger.

"You want to tell your side?" he asked Daniel.

This time he was ready. "Not until I hear his."

"You know mine!" Randy snarled. "You ran into me on purpose!"

"I thought he was going to use his usual turn, but he used mine," Daniel said. "Only he wasn't really prepared for it. Just as he wasn't the first time around when he caused the big pileup. My turn was just right, but he got hung up trying to miss the tires. I had nowhere to go."

"You creep, Bradford! I can outride you anywhere any time, and you know it."

The official interrupted. "I'm disallowing the protest, Mr. Hickock. Even though perhaps Mr. Bradford should have been watching more carefully. He makes a good point about the first lap. I would penalize you for that if someone filed a complaint."

"You mean," Daniel said, "that if I protested Randy because of the first lap crash, he'd be disqualified?"

"Now just wait a minute!" Randy's father shouted. "You can't do this! You can't encourage protests!"

"Don't worry about it," Daniel said. "I can't file a protest because all that crash did was help me. Unless by filing I could switch places with Randy." He was only kidding. But Randy and his father started yelling and swearing and threatening the official.

"I would advise you not to threaten me," the official said. "I know how upset you are. And I also know that young Bradford here was just kidding. He knows as well as you do that the only person who can switch places as the result of a protest is one who was involved in the infraction and was hampered by it."

"That's better," Mr. Hickock said.

"I shouldn't think you would need to file a protest anyway. Your son won, and Bradford finished last. What was the point?"

"To teach him a lesson," Randy said.

"Yes," his father said. "Couldn't he be suspended or something?"

"Perhaps, if the protest had been upheld. However, as I just said, I'm disallowing it."

"Could I file a protest?" Daniel said.

"For what?" the two Hickocks shouted at the same time.

The official raised his hand to silence them. "What would it concern, Mr. Bradford?"

"For getting in my way on the last lap. My bike was damaged because he stepped on it. And I believe I could have won the race otherwise."

"You're kidding!" Randy shouted. "I don't believe this!"

Daniel wasn't totally serious. But he wasn't kidding, either. He didn't know why he had said it. He knew it wouldn't get far. But he just felt the urge to bother Randy and his huffy father some more. "I'm not kidding," he said.

"Disallowed," the official said quickly. "Now I would advise you boys to straighten out your differences at your first opportunity."

Daniel thought about shaking Randy's hand and apologizing for filing a protest. But he was too late. Randy and his father stomped away.

"Never!" Randy said.

"Forget it!" his father said.

9
Good Sport

Daniel dragged his bike, the front wheel off the ground, over to where his family waited. "You want to stay and watch the final, Dan?" his father asked.

"I guess."

After they made sure he was all right and took a close look at his bike, no one said much. Daniel knew they thought he was terribly disappointed. And in a way he was.

He was a little embarrassed that he let himself be pushed into being a bad sport just because Randy and his dad were so mean. But in another way, he felt pretty good. He was learning quickly how this sport worked.

He hadn't expected to make the semifinals, let alone find himself actually fighting for the lead.

He knew that most of his success was because of the big crash on the first lap and his decision to stay back and in the middle for a while.

Now he just needed to put it all together: a strong start, a good turn, a powerful climb up the hill, Randy's technique on the long curve, and careful choices of where to ride. If he could, he knew he could start competing for trophies.

He felt bad about the argument with Randy and with Tom Engle, too. It wasn't the way he wanted to act or be. But he didn't know quite what to do about it. Silently, he prayed and asked for forgiveness and strength to be a better Christian and a better sport. He decided he would talk with Jim about it later.

In the final race for his age group a half hour later, Randy jumped off to an early lead and even improved on Daniel's cornering technique on the first turn. Jim whooped and hollered. Even Mr. Bradford shook his head in disbelief.

Randy had come over the jump low, as usual, and drove into the turn just like Daniel, leaning way to the left. Then, rather than fighting to keep the bike upright, he leaned all the way to the right and kept going.

He had taken the tight turn without slowing down or throwing himself off balance. He was light and relaxed and sped up the hill. He careened down the other side and into his wide turn. By the end of the first lap, he was a full second ahead of the course record for fifteen-years-olds, let alone his own age group.

He picked up more than another second on the second lap. He shattered the course record in front of a screaming crowd. He did a successful, controlled wheelie all the way around the track for a victory lap. Then he held both fists in the air as he coasted to the trophy stand to receive his prize.

For some reason, Daniel felt a little sorry for him. He knew Randy didn't have any real friends. No one liked him. The parents wished he would move up in class or out of the area. Certainly no one was going to beat him in his own age group.

The Bradford family slowly left the racetrack park. Mr. Bradford carried Daniel's bike.

That night Daniel lounged around in his big, fluffy bathrobe after a long, hot bath. The family enjoyed a leisurely cookout. Daniel was a little surprised and confused because no one tried to lecture him. They consoled him some. They told him they were proud of him for the way he had tried. But even when he told the story of his argument with Randy and his half-serious counter-protest, no one said anything.

He decided that maybe they were letting him work it out for himself. The next day in Sunday school and church, it seemed that everything that was taught, preached, talked about, or sung had to do with being kind to others, not returning evil for evil, and all of that.

Daniel had heard it all before, of course. He knew that's the reason he felt a little guilty after his bad encounters the day before. But he thought it was strange that everything that Sunday centered on the way he should treat people who didn't like him. It made him feel restless all day.

The next day, after he got home from work, Jim helped Daniel work on his bike in the garage. For the longest time, the only things Jim talked about were the bike and Daniel's riding. "One thing I want you to work on, Dan, is running up and down the stadium steps at the high school football field."

"Why? I mean, I've seen you do that, but why?"

"It helps a lot of things. Good for your toes, heels, ankles, calf muscles, hamstrings, heart, lungs, stamina, everything. If you use your arms right, it can even be good for them."

"I'll try it if you think it would be good for me."

Jim let Daniel take over working on lubricating the chain and back wheel sprocket. Then he cleaned his hands and wrote out a training plan for the week. When the bike was back in perfect condition, Jim carefully lowered it to the floor and let Daniel ride it slowly in a circle in the garage.

"Perfect," Daniel said. "Now let me see that schedule."

He stood with both feet on the ground and the bike between his legs, reading by the late afternoon sunlight coming through the window. "What's this all about? Run, stop, think, run, stop, think."

"Well, figure it out for yourself. You know what the running is all about. You go up and down the steps at the

51

highest point, then you stop. For resting. Then you think, either while you're resting or while you're running the steps."

"What am I supposed to think about?"

"What do you think?"

"Strategy?" Daniel tried.

"That's part of it. But you've already proved you have a good handle on that."

"The competition?"

"Yes, but you know that, too. Your competition, if you do your best, is Randy and a couple of other top riders. You've proved you're fearless and know when to make your move. You know pretty much what they're going to do. The only thing you don't know is which type of turn Randy will make on the first curve. The second one is always the same."

"Yeah, because there's no better or faster way a person could run that curve."

"Don't be too sure. Anyway, what I'm getting at is that you know how to ride and who you're riding against."

"Then what do I have to think about?"

"Think about those things so they'll be solid in your mind. But you should do the rest of your thinking about what's been on your mind since Saturday."

"Which is?"

"Don't ask me, Daniel. It's your mind. And you haven't said anything."

"But you do know what it is, don't you, Jim?"

"I have a good idea."

"Want to try it out on me?"

Jim sat on the tool bench and sighed. "OK, sure. I think you're a little worried about your feelings toward Tom and Randy. And I also think you're a little woried about what you might have done to them if your mom and dad weren't at that race."

"How did you know that?"

"I just put myself in your place, that's all."

"And you would have popped them one?"

52

"I would have wanted to. Are you afraid of them?"

"I wouldn't want to take them on at the same time, of course."

"Did you remember that Mom and Dad can't make it to the races next weekend?"

Daniel nodded.

"And Yolanda and Maryann can't be there either."

"Just you and me then, Jim?"

"Yeah, but I'm thinking about not coming."

"You're kidding! You wouldn't do that to me, would you?"

"I might."

"How would I get there? It's too far to ride. And I don't like to ride my dirt bike on pavement anyway."

"I would drop you off, Dan. Then you'd be on your own. You'd be doing what's right just because God is there, and not because anybody from your family is there to rat on you."

Daniel didn't know what to think. "I want you there, Jim. I need someone there watching me and helping me. I wouldn't even want to race if you weren't there."

"Are you sure you're not just afraid what kind of person you'd be with no one watching?"

"That might be part of it. But no, that's not all of it. I want to be the way I'm supposed to be. I don't know what Tom or Randy have cooked up for me. And I don't know what I'm supposed to do if they pull something bad. But promise me you'll be there."

"Not yet," Jim said. "Not just yet."

10

Training with Jim

All during the next week, Daniel ran the stadium steps at the high-school football field. At first he thought he was going to die. *And I thought I was in shape,* he said to himself. It took a few days to get used to the strain. And then he started looking forward to the workouts. He could feel his legs getting stronger and his stamina increasing.

And when he finished yard work or a long ride on his ten speed or his dirt bike, he went home and waited for Jim to get off work. Then he trained some more.

Jim coached him on balance and speed and strength and even steering. But most of all, Jim trained him in how he should think and react, especially when bad things happen.

"Did you know," he asked Daniel, "that when you answer an angry person with a soft voice, it's like heaping coals of fire on his head?"

"I've heard that. But what does it mean?"

"It means that it humiliates him even more. He doesn't get his desired response. He's angry; he wants you angry so he can keep yelling. You need to think about how you will react if one of those two boys really tries to hassle you next week. You're ready to race well. You've proved that you can stay with the leaders. And you're working out all week so you'll be ready. But what are you going to do if they attack your mind?"

"My mind?"

"Throw you off by getting you mad."

"Like I did with Randy?"

"Sort of, but you didn't do it on purpose."

"It seemed to help him ride even faster."

"Nah! The only reason he rode faster was because there was no one pressuring him. As soon as he got clear of you, he still had time to mount his bike and stay in front of everybody. When you can do that—and you're the fastest rider anyway—there's no pressure. But what if he had been really angry and had pressure besides?"

"He probably wouldn't have done well. But I don't want to make him mad just to make him do poorly."

"Of course you don't. But be prepared. He and Tom both have threatened you. How are you going to react?"

"I don't know. Are you going to be there?"

"Does it make a difference, Daniel?"

"It might."

"It shouldn't."

"I know. But it might."

"All right, Dan, let's say I was there. How would you act?"

"If what?"

"If, say, Tom does something bad to you. He gets in your way, knocks you over, knocks you out of the race, lies about you, damages your bike?"

"I'd file a protest."

"Is that all?"

"What else is there? I don't think I'd fight him, if that's what you mean."

"I'm not talking about what you wouldn't do. I'm talking about what you *would* do."

"You mean I should thank him or something?" Daniel said.

"I wouldn't go that far."

"Then what?"

"That's up to you. That's something you need to think about and be prepared for. What's the best thing you can do for a person who has badly used you?"

"The Bible says to pray for him. But that doesn't mean out loud or right in front of him, does it?"

"No. But how should you treat a person you're praying for?"

"Well," Daniel said thoughtfully, "you shouldn't. . ."

"Don't tell me what you shouldn't do, Dan. Tell me what you *should* do. I don't expect you to fight the boys even if I'm not there. But you can't just ignore them. You have to respond. And you're not going to pay back evil for evil. So what are you going to do?"

"I don't know," Daniel said. "And it looks like you're not going to tell me."

"You got that right."

"Then how am I supposed to learn?"

"Read your Bible. Pray. Watch Mom and Dad."

"I will, but I still want to know whether you're going to be there Saturday."

"I don't know yet."

"Why not?"

"Because I want you to do this on your own, Daniel. There's nothing I'd rather do than be there and see how you ride. Because I know you'll do your best ever. And I'm curious to know how you'll handle it if you get into a scrape with either Tom or Randy. But I don't want to influence you. I don't want you to do or not do something just because I'm there."

Daniel couldn't argue with that. He had already admitted that Jim's being there might make a difference. He didn't know what kind. But he knew it would make some kind of difference.

Every night during his devotions, Daniel looked up

verses he'd heard about in Sunday school the week before. He was developing a plan. All the while, he was praying that Jim would decide to come to the race.

Friday rolled around. Daniel didn't know which he was more excited about, the races he felt more ready for than ever or the trouble with Randy and Tom, which he also finally felt prepared for.

He didn't even tell Jim what he had decided. Each time Jim asked what he was going to do, he said, "Just show up and find out. I'm ready."

"Ready for what?"

"Ready for anything."

"Sounds interesting."

"Come and see for yourself, Jim."

"I might. I just might."

"Promise?"

"I promise I might. That's all. Can you promise it won't make a difference if I'm there or not?"

Daniel thought a while, then shrugged. "Not really, no. I can't promise that for sure."

"Then I may not decide until tomorrow morning when I drop you off."

That night Daniel prayed again that Jim would decide to stay and watch him. But he felt the prayer was a little selfish. He really had more confidence in his plan if someone were watching. But as Jim told him many times during that week, "Remember, God is watching anyway."

Dan was up very early the next morning. He took a long, slow ride on his ten-speed, just to limber up. The most loosening up he'd get at the track would be a couple of practice laps and some stretching exercises. When he got back, he was ready for a big, hot breakfast. Racing would begin at nine. And all but the finals would be before noon.

"Wish we could be there today, Dan," his father said.

"Me too," he said.

"You ready?"

"Yeah. More than ever." He glanced at Jim, who winked.

"Just do your best, and we'll be proud of you," Mrs. Bradford said. "I know you will."

"I'll try."

Daniel took a long time pulling on his suit that morning. Everything was fresh and clean and bright. He liked the way he looked in green. He prayed silently that God would remind him of everything he had promised to do, both on the track and with Randy and Tom. And he added that he sure would appreciate it if Jim was there.

He surprised Jim by lifting the bike into the back of the station wagon himself. "Getting stronger every day," he said smiling. Jim looked astonished. "Need any help with anything?" Jim laughed.

Neither of them spoke on the way to the track. When they pulled in the gate, Jim stopped before coming to the parking lot. Daniel's heart sank. He opened the door and switched his sneakers for his riding boots. Then he dug his helmet and gloves out of the back seat. He snapped them on while Jim wheeled his bike around.

"We're early," Jim said. "You could get in one of the early practice laps."

"Yeah," Daniel muttered.

"I'll be thinking about you and praying for you," Jim said.

"Sure."

And Jim drove away.

11

Coals of Fire

Daniel could hardly get over his dissappointment that not even Jim would be there that day. He needed someone to talk to, to ride for, to support him. He needed someone behind him while he was racing. And while he was not.

He figured Jim thought he was doing the right thing. But it didn't make Daniel feel any better. He wandered to the track to see who was riding in which heat. Only a few other riders were there.

Daniel read the list of the eight qualifying heats that fed into the quarter finals. Neither Tom nor Randy were in his heat, which didn't surprise him. They weren't riding together in any of the others, either. He wondered when he would face either of them. Quarters. Semifinals. Or finals.

He pushed his bike through the entrance to the track.

One other rider was cruising around slowly. "Hi, Dan!" he called, waving.

Daniel didn't recognize him at first. The rider stopped and took off his helmet, smiling.

"Oh, hi, Mike!" Dan said. "Here early, huh?"

"Yeah. I'd like to make the quarter finals just once. Bet you'll be in the finals today."

"How do you figure?"

"Oh, everybody can tell how much better you've got. You made the semi's last week, didn't you?"

Daniel nodded.

"Lotta people think you might have beaten Randy if he hadn't slowed you down and then stepped on your wheel."

"People noticed that?"

"Everybody. Bet you'd like to get your hands on him."

"Nah. Wouldn't mind beating him in a race though, fair and square. How's the track?"

"Softer than last week, that's for sure. I think they wetted it down about an hour ago. And it's not supposed to get very hot today."

"That's good. It might mean slower times. But at least you won't get hurt if you fall."

"Yeah, unless you get run over or somebody pushes you through the fence. Like you'd like to do to Randy."

"No, I wouldn't."

"I would."

"I'd better get riding. See you. And good luck."

The track felt firm but soft, too, not rock hard like the week before. Daniel got excellent traction, but he didn't go fast enough to fly over the jump. He just went up it and rolled down. It was steeper this week for some reason. Work had been done on the whole course. He knew why. The best finishers in each age category would be selected for a traveling team. They would have uniforms and jackets and everything. They would get to go on trips all over the state to compete in other cities. Daniel hadn't even been able to hope for something like that until now.

He slowly maneuvered through the tight turn. He noticed that the dirt was loose around it. That would help his type of turn. Randy's, too. He also knew that after the early heats the track would firm up more and ruts would appear. The type of riding he was doing on it wouldn't affect it at all. But when there were twenty to thirty riders at a time,

60

going as fast as they could, the patterns would soon be cut deeply into the surface.

To loosen himself up and see how the bike was handling, he stood and pushed his way up the hill. He kept his speed constant as he came down the other side. He didn't want to race around the curve with the top soil so loose. So he coasted.

It felt good to feel the air sneaking under his helmet around his neck. He wished he could take the helmet and gloves off and really feel the wind. But he didn't want to get used to riding without them.

He rolled out the entrance of the track and over toward the registration table to get his number and pay his money. There he saw Randy's father.

"Hi, Mr. Hickock," he said, sticking out his hand.

The man slowly shook it. "Yeah, hi, kid. What's happening?"

"Not much. Where's Randy?"

"Making some last minute adjustments on the bike. He'll be along."

"Well, good luck today."

The man looked surprised. "Yeah, OK, thanks." He walked away.

"Tell Randy I said good luck, too!" Daniel called after him. He knew Mr. Hickock had heard him, but the man didn't turn around.

Later he saw Tom Engle. "Hey, Tom, how's it going?"

Tom responded by swearing.

"Hope you have a good day of racing," Daniel said. "Been on the track yet?"

"What's it to you, Bradford?"

"Just wondering. I was out. Feels pretty good. They've been working on it. The jump's so high you can't even see over it."

"That so? Guess I'd better watch out for you then, shouldn't I? You'll probably fall over and sit there waiting for people to run into you."

"No, I won't. I'll be real careful today. I hope you have a good day of racing and that you make the traveling team."

"Don't worry, I will if I can keep out of your way. Don't you count on making it."

"Well, I'm going to do my best. But I'm probably not that good yet. Good luck, Tom."

Tom sneered at him. "Buzz off, Bradford."

Daniel wished more than ever that Jim was still around. He didn't even have anyone to guard his bike while he watched the preliminary heats of the younger kids' races. So, he just stood next to the fence with his bike right next to him. It was lonely.

It was also interesting. He watched the younger boys and girls. He tried to pick out the best racers, the smartest and toughest kids, and who he thought would win the finals in each category. Finally, it was time for his own qualifying heat.

He knew a couple of the kids in his heat. But most were kids he had just seen around. He was placed near the front. He wasn't sure why. Maybe just luck. He was surprised how easy it was this week.

The jump was scary, it was so high. He felt as if he were going over backward when he finally banged to the ground. He was in third place. He wasn't really in a position to try his fancy move in the tight turn. He just slowed and went around it like everyone else, counting on his new leg strength to push him up the hill. He had to finish in the top five.

He was still in third coming down the other side when he decided to open up and try to win his heat. He hadn't really considered that before they started. But he felt so fresh and strong now that he felt it was worth a try.

By the time he hit the jump for the second time he had a solid lead. But the jump threw him sideways. He was certain he was going to tumble over. He yanked on the bike while still in the air, hoping to hit straight.

He was still sideways when he came down. The jump

had cost him so much time that two racers nearly caught him. He had hoped to have enough of a lead going into the tight turn to try his specialty, but they were too close.

He went through it the normal way and was pleased to realize that he still felt strong. Plus he felt so good being in the lead without the benefit of any accidents or luck that it charged him up. He stood and pushed hard up and down the hill and around the big curve.

He almost lost it at one point coming out of the curve. He felt he was going as fast as Randy ever had, but he just raised up in his seat and let the wind slow him down. When he went across the finish line he was almost crying. He was leading by twenty feet, had improved on his best time, and hadn't been happier in years.

And, oh, how he wished Jim could have been there! Or anyone from the family. He headed back to his spot by the fence and sat down to enjoy the feeling. A couple of his friends and their parents came by to congratulate him. Tom and Randy just happened by, too.

"Enjoy it while it lasts, loser," Randy said.

Tom just laughed.

Within a few minutes, each of them had won their own qualifying heats. Randy set another record. But it was only for twelve-year-olds because the track wasn't hard and fast enough for him to break any of the better records.

Tom had won his heat by almost fifty feet. He looked better than Daniel had ever seen him.

Daniel looked forward to the quarter finals, wondering whether he'd face either of his enemies there.

12

The Soft Answer

Daniel was so excited about having finally won a race that he started a little too fast in his quarter final. Neither Tom nor Randy were in his heat. So he tried to get way out ahead.

His trouble started early. He flew even farther sideways over the jump. He had to put both feet out and come to a stop before getting going again. At least he hadn't fallen.

But by the time he got to the first curve, the tight one, he was in last place and was able to practice his favorite move. It worked perfectly and put him right back in the race. By the time he came down the big hill and went around the wide curve, he was back with the leaders.

The problem was that he couldn't go high on the outside because there was too much traffic. He took the jump very slowly and carefully the second time. So he waited until he got to the wide curve the second time and made his big move there. By then, it was just Daniel and the two leaders out ahead of everyone.

He handled the curve well and moved into a tie for first. But he was still on the outside. And the two leaders easily kept him out there by legally drifting his direction as they fought for the finish line.

A strong third looked good on his record. But he still thought he could have won it if he hadn't done so poorly on the jump. He settled in near the fence again to watch the other categories and the other quarter finals in his age group.

Tom and Randy were in the same quarter final. *This should be interesting,* Daniel thought. And it was. Randy took the treacherous jump easily the first time over. And he let Tom get ahead of him going into the first turn.

Tom took it the normal way, just ahead of Randy, who had slowed enough that he was barely leading the rest of the pack. Randy charged into the turn, hit the rut on purpose, and shot out in front of everyone else.

Most of them went down or slid off the track. Randy quickly flew off in pursuit of Tom. That eliminated a couple of very good racers who might have beaten Tom, even if they wouldn't have threatened Randy.

As soon as Randy got near Tom, Tom moved inside and let him pass. Then he followed Randy down the hill and around the sweep, heading into the second lap. No one had been hurt in the early fall. So the better riders regained the lead of the second pack. But no one could catch the two leaders.

Randy slowed enough so that Tom was right behind him. And the winning time was about what Tom would have run by himself. It was clearly a case of teamwork keeping Tom in the competition. But nothing either of them had done had been illegal, since Randy didn't hit anyone.

It was bad sportsmanship for Tom to let Randy take the lead. It was bad sportsmanship for Randy not to ride his fastest once he had it. But there were no rules against that. Daniel was disgusted. But he was running over in his mind how he might ride if he faced either of them in the semifinal.

He faced Tom in the next race. Daniel carefully surveyed the field and realized that he was going to have a tough time qualifying. At least he had done well enough that he was not one of the slower ones who had to face Randy and the other top leaders in the semi's. That was a good sign.

But he knew there were at least a half dozen riders in this race who had beaten his best time. It was going to take everything he had to make the top five. He wasn't sure whether to key in on Tom and just try to beat him. He figured that if he did, he'd likely make the top five. Or should he just go out the best he knew how and try to win the thing?

He decided on the latter. Yet he could tell from the beginning that Tom was out to get him. It was obvious that Tom cared more about causing trouble for Daniel than about qualifying for the finals.

Right from the start, Tom aimed at Daniel's bike. Daniel let him pass quickly over the first jump. He knew how difficult he himself had found it. But Tom handled it fairly well. In the first turn, Tom slowed down sharply, and Dan had to swerve to miss him as he went by.

Then Tom caught up to him. He got ahead by half a bike's length and moved right into Daniel. Their bikes actually bumped, and Daniel yelled, "Hey!"

"Hey, yourself!" Tom yelled and steered toward him again.

Daniel took to the inside and sprinted away up the hill and down the other side. Luckily the leaders had taken an inside track, too. He moved to the outside at top speed and swept around the way Randy did. He quickly caught them and left Tom far behind.

But the leaders moved to the outside again as they got on the straightaway, and Daniel was boxed in. He fell in behind them, only to find Tom right next to him again. This time he didn't want Tom to beat him over the jump and get to the tight curve first. If he could hold him off, he knew he could stay out of trouble until the end. All of his endurance training was paying off.

He lost a little nerve as they headed for the jump at the same time. Tom was on the inside. Daniel hesitated slightly, and they flew over together, straight and low, landing nicely. They were dead even. But Daniel had the advantage of being on the outside.

He raced for the curve, beat Tom to it, and faked as if he was going to use his usual turn. Tom backed off to avoid hitting him. Daniel made a normal turn, leaving Tom behind. He raced as hard as he could to keep Tom from hassling him anymore, and it worked. He finished fourth, Tom fifth. They both qualified for the finals. For Daniel, it was the first time ever, and he felt great.

At the end of the heat, as they wheeled off the track, Daniel held out his hand to Tom. "Nice race, Tom. Congratulations. See you in the final."

Tom just stared at him and went the other way. Daniel saw Tom and Randy talking together as they watched the other races, waiting for the final. If only Jim were here!

Daniel ate his lunch alone at the concession stand. Tom and Randy walked right by him without noticing him. Daniel heard Randy saying, "No! No tricks this time. I'm going for the record and that's it. If you can stay with me, fine— you'll get second place. But don't count on it."

Daniel felt tired but eager to get racing agian. He didn't consider winning, although he was going to do his best. He would be in the front row right next to Randy, based on his super time in the qualifying heat. Tom would be directly behind Randy.

When it was finally time to race, Daniel's heart was pounding. "Good luck," he said to the boys on either side of him and behind. Some gave him the thumbs-up sign. Others ignored him. Tom gave him the cut-throat sign.

Randy lifted his helmet so he could be heard. "If you know what's good for you, Bradford, you'll stay out of my way."

Daniel nodded, but only to indicate that he'd heard, not that he was going to obey. He wanted to say, "You don't scare me," but he didn't. For one thing, Randy did scare him a little. But he certainly wasn't going to drop back on purpose.

In fact, knowing Randy's strategy, he decided to try to stay with him for as long as he could. Maybe he could finish in the top three if he set his sights on the best.

When the gun sounded, Daniel couldn't believe how fast Randy started. He was out and away from everyone before they even hit the dip in front of the jump. Daniel was pumping as hard as he could. He quickly moved over so he was directly behind Randy. That was the best position, he decided. Someone else would have to be awfully fast to get ahead of him.

Randy must have lost concentration or was going too fast. When he went over the jump, he didn't stay low as he usually did. He flew way up in the air and turned completely sideways. He frantically tried to straighten himself out. But he landed just as he had turned. His tires dug into the dirt and stopped.

Daniel had remembered to keep his body forward and his head low. As he came down, he was looking right into Randy's terrified eyes, peeking out of his Plexiglas face shield.

Daniel's bike landed right on top of Randy's. They both went down in a heap. Daniel jumped up quickly. He knew that eight more speeding bikes had moved right into line behind them and couldn't see that they had fallen.

In a split second, he tried and failed to drag Randy out of the way. Randy was caught under both bikes. Daniel jumped in front of Randy and stood, waving toward the outside for the riders to swerve if they could.

The biker who had been on Daniel's right at the start jerked his bike away in the air and fell. But he missed both of them. The next one over the jump was Tom. He, too, had gone too high. He didn't turn, however, and came down straight onto Daniel.

His chain sprocket caught Daniel's helmet and cracked the face mask. The chain tore the sleeve from Daniel's suit and ripped through his glove and the back of his hand. Tom flew off the bike and stumbled into the dirt. Several more

68

bikers came over the rise, smashing into the three bikes.

When the dust had cleared, Tom walked away unhurt. Randy limped away on a twisted ankle. And Daniel lay on his stomach with a sore jaw, wrenched neck, nicked ear, sliced hand, and a bruised hip.

Officials immediately stopped the race and ran to help. Daniel was the only seriously hurt rider, though several bikes were out of commission.

Daniel's bike had somehow escaped damage. But Randy's was crunched badly.

Randy was swearing. "My bike's shot!" he wailed.

"Use mine," Daniel said. "I can't ride anymore. Use it."

Randy stared at him. "Are you serious, Bradford? This accident was my fault, and you're gonna let me use your Malta?"

Daniel nodded as he was led away. A doctor was already looking at his hand. "This will require stitches," he said. "Let's get it cleaned up."

"Can't I watch this race first?" he asked.

"All right, but then we have to go."

They restarted the final, and Randy won easily. Tom finished sixth.

While Daniel was in the first aid tent, Randy and his father came by to bring his bike back. "Thanks, Dan," Randy said, shaking his hand.

"Yes," Mr. Hickock said. "I don't know what to say."

Suddenly, Jim came running up. "Dan, are you all right?"

"What are you doing here?"

"I've been here all day, Dan," he said, putting his arm around Daniel. "I saw and heard everything, kid. Am I proud of you!"

69

Moody Press, a ministry of the Moody Bible Institute, is designed for education, evangelization, and edification. If we may assist you in knowing more about Christ and the Christian life, please write us without obligation: Moody Press, c/o MLM, Chicago, Illinois 60610.